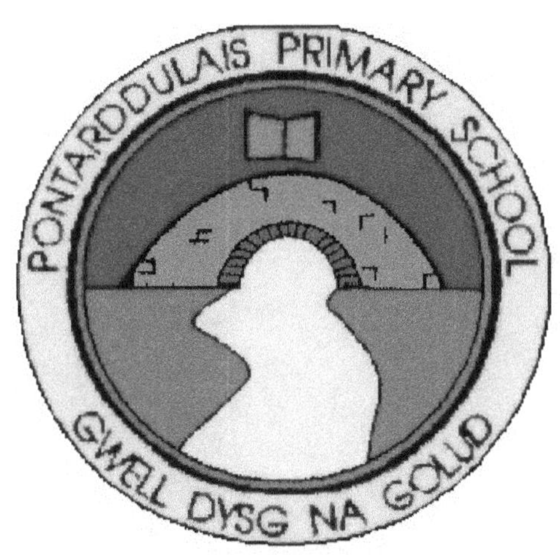

Pontarddulais Primary School

2015 Anthology

Written by the Creative Writing Club

Edited by Mr. Fox

CONTENTS:

ACKNOWLEDGMENTS

Thank you to the children who took part in the Creative

Writing Club and all the hard work you have put into this.

You are all very talented writers and I am proud to have

done this for you.

Well done.

<u>1 / The Dog with no Voice.</u>

<u>By Lauren Williams</u>

There once lived a princess whose words were pure poetry. She amused the court with her witty, rhyming verse, yet her kind and thoughtful words made her popular with all. She had beautiful, shining blonde hair and was very beautiful to behold. It was said she could even charm the birds from the trees.

One day, she was walking in a forest with loads of guards for her protection, when she came upon an old lady with a huge bundle on her back.

"Let me help," offered the princess.

The old woman accepted the offer. With a smile, the princess took the bag and walked along beside the woman, the guards following close behind. They chatted away talking about where they lived, what they did, and before long they had reached the old lady's door.

Now, the old lady, who was really a witch, had been listening entirely to the princess's words.

What a fine voice she has, the witch thought to

herself, I would like my daughter to speak like that, and then maybe she could find herself a handsome, wealthy man. Then we would be rich for ever more.

"You must be thirsty form all that walking," the witch said to the princess as she led her in. "Let me give you something to quench your thirst to repay you for your kindness. A bit of squash, is that all right?"

The princess gratefully accepted, unaware that the guards outside were placed into a sleeping spell, and was given a delicious drink. Without wasting a drop, she drained the entire drink. But in the drink was a spell.

Suddenly, she noticed that she was getting smaller and smaller. She looked down at her hands and feet. They were no longer hands and feet, they were now four hairy paws. She turned in horror and saw a shaggy tail. What came out of her mouth was no longer her sweet singing voice, but a loud bark.

Whilst this was happening, the witch turned to her daughter, who was quietly hiding in the cupboard:

"It has gone wrong my dear. You cannot have the princess's voice. A spell is protecting her, by someone else, so that if anyone tries to take her voice they will turn into a dog like her."

"So we have to give her voice back?" asked the witch's daughter with a quiet voice as she walked out from hiding, a beautiful girl herself.

"I will give the voice back."

Using her magic, the witch created another spell. Suddenly, the princess was back to normal size and she could talk again.

"Thank you," the princess said. "But why?"

"We thought if we stole your voice for my daughter, she would be able to find a handsome man to marry her."

"She does not need my voice, she is beautiful and has a lovely voice herself."

"Thank you," the witch replied. "You better get back home," and as she said this she woke the guards up outside.

Not wanting the witch and her daughter to get into trouble, the princess said nothing to the guards, and ordered for them to take her home back to the castle.

When they arrived back at the castle, the princess was shocked to see standing there the witch and her daughter.

"Why are you here?" the princess asked in a confused way.

"I've come to see you," her daughter replied in her quiet voice.

"But why?" the princess asked.

"We've come to say sorry for real because we didn't mean it in the first please. Forgive us, we beg you plea…" growing upset and afraid.

"Don't worry, I forgive you," replied the princess, reaching out for the girl's shoulders.

"Why?"

"Because you are poor and afraid,' she answered with a kind voice. "I invite you to live with me and my family together.

The princess guided the girl and her mother into the castle, showing them to a long corridor filled with doors.

"Let me show you your room, your room is on the left," the princess said to the girl, and then to the witch, "and your room is on the right. If you walk this way is the garden, the garden is big so you and your daughter can play together.

"Here are some toys for you to play with, so see you later."

In the afternoon, the witch and her daughter were invited for tea, where they had spaghetti bolognaise. After the meal, they all went off to bed, the little girl went to sleep straightaway. As for the witch, who showed she was really a kind, nice old lady, stayed awake, unable to believe all this that had happened, eventually going to sleep.

The End

<u>2 / The Wolf and the Two Boys.</u>

<u>By James Llewellyn</u>

One day, a little boy called Joe was going for a walk through a quiet and light wood. As he walked through the thick woods, he heard a weird noise. It sounded like something scratching a tree!

Joe turned around and saw a tree with a mark on it.

Joe had a feeling that he had seen a mark like that before on a TV programme. It looked a lot like a wolf had done it. Joe was only five years old and he had never seen a wolf before, and he didn't want to either.

Joe went home trying to forget about the wolf mark.

"What's for tea?" asked Joe curiously as he got home.

"Fish fingers, beans and chips," replied Joe's big brother, James, who was much older than Joe.

Joe loved fish fingers so he was rather pleased to hear that information.

"Tea's ready," said mum from the kitchen.

So Joe made his way to the living room. When Joe got to the living room, James was already sitting at the table ready to have tea. The table was laid and set very nicely.

After tea, Joe went over to James and asked:

"Are you scared of wolves?"

"No!" replied James. "Why?"

"BECAUSE I was walking through the woods at something like 11 O'clock and I turned to see a tree with a wolf mark on it. ill you help me find out what it is?" asked Joe.

"Yes!" said James joyfully. "I will help you track down that wolf!"

On the way to the forest, they bumped into Curious Cameron, who was very curious as all of you can probably tell! Curious Cameron stared at them for a moment.

"Where are you going?" he asked stubbornly.

"We are going to my Grandma's," lied James.

"I thought your Grandma lives miles away?" said Cameron.

"She's moved house because, um…um…um, because of an earthquake," replied James.

"I watch the news every morning of my life and I haven't heard anything about an earthquake! Doesn't matter, off you two go!" said curious Cameron.

"Finally!" said James. "I thought that guy would never leave us alone!"

"At least we can get to the woods" said Joe.

James and Joe had been walking for half an hour and they were tired.

"Look!" said Joe, "There it is!"

"Woohhh!, that is awesome," said James, "how did you find it?"

"Well, I heard a noise behind me so obviously I turned around and saw this tree and I was sure I had seen it before! Do you remember from that TV show?"

Now, something that James and Joe didn't know was that Curious Cameron was watching them the whole time!

"What is this?" asked Curious Cameron.

"This, this….um…..we….LET'S GET HIM!!!!!" screamed

James and Joe together.

"Ahhhhhhhgggggg!" shrieked Curious Cameron, and he sped off.

"That's the last of him" said James.

"I don't think we will see him again" said Joe.

James and Joe hated Curious Cameron. They hated him even more than earthquakes destroying everything, an alien invasion or breaking both arms and legs at the same time. So, everyone, you can tell how much the boys hated Curious Cameron.

The next day, James and Joe went to school rather worried that Curious Cameron would tell someone. And that's exactly what he had done. Since Curious Cameron was so stupid, he had told his mum, who was quite soft and let him get away with anything……even flooding the house!

That is just one example of how stupid Curious Cameron is!!

James had just finished double maths and he was outside playing. Then, James saw some footprints leading to a snow mountain close by.

James and Joe followed the prints. (Did I forget to tell you that Joe was playing with James and Joe decided to follow James to the mountain?) Anyway, let's get back to the story shall we?

James and Joe followed the tracks until they reached the mountain. It only took for a few minutes for them to get there.

Then Joe said: "Look, it's a cave!"

"Do you think that cave belongs to the wolf?" asked James.

"Yes I do" replied Joe. "Let's take a look."

James and Joe slowly walked over to the cave and there they heard a noise.

"Hiss, hiss, hiss," went the noise.

That sounds like a snake, thought James and Joe.

"Hiss!" went the noise again.

Then, a long green tail stuck out of the cave.

"Errr!" said Joe.

"Come out already!" said James bravely.

Suddenly, a huge five metre, green snake slithered

out of the cave.

Luckily, James knew about snakes and how to tame one, so he did! Then the snake left them alone.

"Look!" said Joe. "More footprints."

So James and Joe once again followed them. Joe didn't like the snow mountain, in fact he was scared of it.

"Oh my God!" said Joe. "Look… it is the snake again!"

"Why the heck are you so excited about that stupid snake?" asked James angrily.

Joe said nothing.

Suddenly, a wolf pounced out and landed on top of James. It dug its claws into him!

"AAAARRRGGG!!!!!!!!!" screamed James.

The snake appeared and bit the wolf. The wolf was still alive and he ran away.

James and Joe ran home.

"Can we go to Grandma and Grandpa's house?" Joe asked mum when they got home.

"Look at the state of you James!" said mum.

"Oh… what, this… It's just tomato sauce" replied

James.

"Fine, I believe you and yes you can go to your Grandparents" said Mum.

"Thanks!" said the two boys.

Mum drove them over Grandma and Grandpa's house. It was supposed to take ages to get there...but no! It only took a few minutes to get there. James and Joe loved going to Grandma and Grampa's house and hearing their interesting tales even though the house was old and messy!

"Hello boys and how are you doing today?" said Grandma in her sweet old voice.

"We're doing fine thank you very much, how about you?"

"Oh yes, I'm having a good day" Grandma was a very nice woman (and to be honest, she is the best artist I have ever seen!).

"Come in, come in" said Grandma. "How about some coffee?"

"No thank-you Grandma" replied the boys together.

Grandma fell silent for a moment, so James and Joe

went to see their Grandpa.

"Grandpa," James asked, "Haven't you mentioned seeing a wolf before?"

"Yes! Yes!" interrupted Grandpa excitedly. "I know what you are going to say…you've seen a wolf too haven't you?"

"Yes!" replied the boys.

"The day I saw a wolf was just terrible. I had to shoot it and a poor girl down," sobbed Grandpa. "That wolf had tore someone to shreds so I had no choice. Be careful of wolves! I don't want that happening to you special boys!"

The next day, when they got home, the two boys went to search for the wolf again as Grandpa's story had really got them thinking!

James and Joe tracked the wolf's paw prints down to a stream.

There, they saw the wolf. It stood there drinking water. He was black and scary. Suddenly, he turned and pounced at the two boys, but James and Joe managed to dive out of the way in time and....the wolf fell into the stream.

Sparks started to shoot out of it and the wolf made a strange buzzing and beeping noise.

"Oh my gosh!" screeched James. "That wolf is a robot!"

The boys pulled the broken robot wolf from the stream. Underneath the wolf's fur they found a small sign which said:

Invented by Cameron

The boys were shocked and they dragged the robot wolf all the way to Cameron's house. When Cameron answered the door, he gaped at the two boys holding his robot wolf.

"Why did you invent this wolf and frighten us?" demanded James.

Cameron began to sob.

"Well I did it because I was scared at night and I thought I would build the wolf to protect me, then I just used it as a joke on you and Joe. I'm very sorry for scaring you and spying on you too! Please can we become friends?"

James and Joe looked at each other for a moment, no real harm had been done throughout all this.

"Yes!" they said together, "Why not, who knows what other adventures we can have!"

The End.

<u>3 / A Legend's Day.</u>

<u>By Tomas Carr</u>

CHAPTER 1

Once upon a time, there was a fifteen-year-old boy called Jamie. Jamie loved to play with his friends and go to school. Many thought him a cute boy with peach skin, always wearing blue jeans red stripy t-shirt.

But most of all, Jamie loved to read. His favourite book was called Some Legends and Some Enemies. On page one; there was information about a Legend called John. Jamie believed in the Legends, that they were real, and so called John's name.

The next day, the Legend John came alive. Jamie could not believe it, this was the best day of his life. He was so happy he took billions of pictures and put all of the pictures in his bedroom and he almost fainted. When he went to bed, Jamie thought it was a dream, but when he woke up the following morning and saw John, he almost fainted again.

However, a day later an Enemy, by the name of Henry, appeared. Henry tried to destroy Jamie's street. He horrified the townspeople and destroyed everything in sight.

To fight him, Jamie was given fire and ice superpowers by John, but Henry flew away when he saw this.

The next day, Jamie woke up and John wasn't there. Jamie thought John was having breakfast but John wasn't there. He was out, fighting Henry. John won and Henry was victorious.

Then, another Enemy came. This one was called the Man in a Suit. He attacked the universe with rockets he had made and failed because John defeated the Man in a Suit. However, during the battle, John died.

CHAPTER 2

The next year, another Legend came to Jamie. This Legend was named Bob and he protected the universe with his mighty fire and ice powers.

In horror, he saw a load of holes on the planets that were left by the Man in a Suit's rockets and Henry.

Wanting to know more, Jamie looked up on the internet searched for Henry and the Man in a Suit, but nothing about them. Jamie grew scared, but then Bob said something to help him.

'I am the best legend you will ever meet. John was a test to see if you believed in him or not. I am the other Legend and will save you from anything or anyone because I am Bob, the greatest superhero you will meet and will save you from disasters. Not even Mother Nature can stop me. The Queen of Legends called me to protect you Jamie.

'You are the lucky one. Millions of people your age have died by starvation, hurricane and everything like that you will never die.'

The next day, another Enemy came to destroy Bob. This Enemy was named Sir Punchalot.

'I WILL DESTRY YOU BOB,' the Enemy roared.

CHAPTER 3

A great battle happened, frightening the people of Pontarddulais. Thankfully, Sir Punchalot was defeated.

However, a familiar evil returned.

Henry arrived back at earth and tried to destroy it. Fortunately, another Legend also came. A Legend named Jeff, and he stopped Henry because of his laser and ice breath. But then they saw the Man in a Suit destroy the USA, whilst eating chocolate and chips.

Suddenly, an eclipse happened. Blinding many people. But it did not end. The Enemies sent tornadoes, destroying many homes, and any harmed returned as zombies.

Luckily, the zombies were destroyed by another Legend, one called Leonardo. Leonardo had ice breath and laser eyes and he could fly and wore blazing blue armour. With the other Legends and Jamie, all zombies were removed and the two enemies were finally defeated. With everything returned to normal and peace restored, everyone was able to live happily ever after.

THE END.

24

4 / A Fox's Tale.

By Alisha Thomas

Once upon a time, there was a Mother Fox. She had seven cubs and theienames were Skipper, Chip, Jesse, Rose, Pop, Flow and me, Whitetail. Jesse was the oldest out all the cubs and I was the youngest.

Mum always had one rule for us. She always said 'never go past the lake because hunters hunt there'. However, Jesse always disobeyed mum's orders but this time she went to far.

Let me tell you how I saved my family and how Jesse became so naughty and mischeivios.

Jesse was big and cuddly, but she was not what she seemed. Pop was playful, fun and unique; she was the best sis you could ever have! Skipper was a tuff and funny. Flow was fluffy, cute and adorable. Chip was nice and kind, the nicest brother ever! Rose was a big diva, but she could be normal when she wanted to.

The terrible events all started at school on Jesse's birthday. She was 2 fox years old and a new fox came to school. Her name was Foxy. All boy foxes loved her but I loved her the most. Once I even got her flowers secretly! Anyway, Foxy came to school and Jesse was not impressed at all because she was the most popular fox in the school. Now, Foxy was the most popular.

When Jesse met Foxy, she put on the pretended nice act; everyone knew she was faking it but Foxy didn't. I tried to tell her but Foxy didn't listen to me so I knew Jesse could pretend to like her and then I herd Foxy talking to Jesse.

So I went into class, luckily we were in the same class, and it is wet break and that was good. I would be able to have a chat with Foxy and tell her how I felt about her. But she might just think I was joking, but I am still going to try.

However, just as I was about to talk to her, I saw she was going out with Chip one of my big brothers!

I was so upset that Foxy was going out with one of my big brothers.

So, after school I hid behind the big oak tree that we called Big Oak. So I hid behind Big Oak so Chip could not see me.

"Whitetail were are you?" said Chip.

He could not find me so he went home. When Chip and the rest of the gang, and before Foxy went home, I got to catch her but in the end I got her.

" Foxy, Foxy wait! I need to tell you something."

"What whitetail?" asked Foxy.

"I need to tell you something about Chip and Jesse and they are not what they seem Foxy. Jesse is very selfish. As for Chip, oh don't get me started."

"Why tell me this?" said Foxy.

"Because ... Okay, I'll tell you. He is gross, pathetic and mean."

"Oh," said Foxy. "So now I've heard all of that, I don't won't to go out with Chip any more."

"Good!" I said to Foxy.

"Whitetail, can I tell you a secret?"

"What is the secret Foxy?"

"I love you!"

Suddenly, Foxy kissed me on the lips.

I have always dreamed about Foxy kissing me but

when I dream about it I never thought of it like that be

for.

The next day, Foxy and I were walking thorough the
wood. Just before we got home Foxy heard a noise:

BANG BANG BANG!

"Guns!" shouted Foxy.

"It sounds like hunters are coming for us." I said.

So we ran and ran and ran, hoping that they wouldn't
catch us. At the house it was all fine until they heard
the banging. My mom went out to see what was going on,
but the hunters were waiting. Mother Fox was kidnapped
by the hunters.

When Foxy and I got to my house, mum was gone.

"Where is mum?" I asked Flow.

"She went to see what the noise was," said Flow.

"Oh no!" said Foxy and I.

"The hunters have got mum" said Flow.

"We've got to stop them before it is to late." I said.

So we ran to where the hunters kept the forest
animals. In half an hour we got there, sneaking in whilst

the hunters were sleeping, and we saw MUM!

"Mum are you ok?" I said.

"Yes I am fine, but you need to get out of here before the hunters see you trying to help me. If they do, they will kill you. So go!" said mum.

I just looked at mum and said:

"I'm not leaving without you!"

Being very quiet, I untied mum from the pit. Then, Foxy heard footsteps.

"Oh no it's the hunters again!" said Foxy.

We left in minutes. We ran past the hunters, they didn't even see us as we kept to the shadows! So like this, hiding in the shadows, we got home safely and we were all reunited.

Three fox years later, Foxy and I married and had 2 cubs, a boy and a girl. The boy cub's name was Oliver and the girls was Amelia. Them two cub are so naughty but they can be good.

Sometimes ...

<u>5 / The Secret Puppy.</u>

<u>By Megan Goodall</u>

Chapter 1: Flower.

Once upon a time, there was a little girl called Megan. She dreamed of having a puppy. Megan had long brown hair and blue sparkly eyes, and she had wanted a puppy so bad. Her grandparents had a dog and it was the only thing that understood her. But her parents always said no. They were too busy and didn't have any time to go running around a park after a puppy.

Megan was very sad because she couldn't have a puppy. Every day, she went for a walk in the park across the road to sit on her favorite bench.

One day, as she sat down on her bench, sulking, she saw something, in a hole under a tree. Nestled in the hole was a beautiful German shepherd puppy. It had heard her sobbing and so slowly came out to look.

Megan was sitting on the grass now to get a closer look. She had a look to see if the puppy had a collar so she could return the little puppy. But when she looked there was no collar.

"So," she said to the puppy, "I'm going to take you home with me, but you need to hide."

So then Megan hid the little puppy behind her cardigan and carried the puppy back home.

Once she got to her house she slipped through the fence and went through the back door and went upstairs into her bedroom. She was very lucky because everyone was in the kitchen. Megan found a tennis ball in her bedroom and she also found an old baby blanket. She wrapped up the little puppy and gave it the tennis ball to play with. She checked if it was a boy or a girl.

Megan was in luck, it was a girl; she decided to call her Flower.

Chapter 2: Megan's Best Friend.

After a while, Megan's mum called her down for tea.

"I'll be back soon and I'll bring you a biscuit," Megan said to Flower.

Megan put Flower down on her bed and went downstairs for tea. Flower didn't like it on her own so she slid down the side of the bed. Then she started to slowly go downstairs.

Once she got down, she trotted into the kitchen where everybody was eating. Megan turned around to get some juice, then she saw Flower. It was lucky that she had finished her tea, she quickly ran over to Flower while her family were still busy eating, and carried her upstairs to her bedroom without anyone seeing.

Then, Megan's mum shouted for her again:

"Megan! Come down here this instant because your friend Aimee will be here in 5 minutes!"

No! Megan had forgot her friend, Aimee, was coming over for a week while her parents were in Spain.

Ding a ling ding a ling went the doorbell.

Oh no, Megan thought, it's Aimee, I've got to hide Flower. She quickly hid Flower under her bed. Then Aimee came bounding in and ran up the stairs carrying bags and a suitcase. As soon as she got into Megan's bedroom she started to unpack. Then she had a sniff of the air and said:

"Come on little puppy Wuppy."

"What are you doing calling for a puppy?" asked Megan acting innocent.

"Because I can smell dog hair."

Chapter 3: The Reveal of the Secret.

Megan knew that she had to say now or never. She was going to have to face having the puppy taken away.

"It's true," said Megan, "I've been keeping a puppy here since lunch time."

"Can I see the puppy?"

"OK, but you have to promise me that you won't tell anybody. Because otherwise I'll have her taken off me forever.

"What's its name?" asked Aimee.

"Flower, she's a German Shepherd," Megan said. "Flower, come on Flower."

Then, from under her bed, Flower came sprinting out, licking Megan and Aimee all over their faces.

"She's so cute," Aimee squealed

"8 o'clock girls, time for bed," Megan's mum shouted from downstairs.

They put Flower on the toilet seat and started to brush their teeth. After they had brushed their teeth, they asked her mum to leave until they had got changed. After her mum had gone downstairs they carried Flower into Megan's room and put her on the bed and started to put their nighties on.

"I want to be a vet when I'm older," said Megan.

"And I'll be your veterinary nurse," added Aimee. "I love animals."

After a conversation which went on for at least 10 minutes, they got into their sleeping bags. With Flower sleeping on top of Megan, and then they fell fast asleep.

Chapter 4: Sadness

The girls woke up put on their dressing gowns and slippers and got a biscuit from Aimee's lunch box and fed it to Flower. Megan and Aimee told Flower that they would be back after some breakfast.

They ran downstairs as fast as they could and sat at the table ready to eat. Megan's brother Ben had already eaten most of his. After Megan's mum had put a bowl of cereal in front of them, Ben said "loser bones" which Megan and Aimee found quite mean.

Whilst all that was happening, Megan's mum went to get the letters because the postman had just been. There was a yellow letter on the floor.

Megan's mum knew something was wrong for the letter was yellow. Megan's mum picked up the letter and read what it said. Megan's mum came into the kitchen and burst into tears. They all asked her what was wrong.

"It's your parents," Megan's mum said to Aimee. "They're … dead. On the way to Spain the plane crashed and there were no survivors. You have to come and live with us".

Aimee burst into tears and ran up-stars with Megan behind.

When Megan quickly followed her, she found Aimee in her bedroom. Aimee was on her knees holding Flower, sobbing as she said:

"Mum, Dad I'm sorry for everything I did wrong just please don't leave me now, not now."

Megan burst into tears hugging Aimee. She didn't like seeing her friend sad, especially her best friend.

Chapter 5: A New Beginning

It had been two days since the news, and school had rung to say that they could have a week off school to get everything sorted. They had brought all the things that Aimee wanted to keep into Megan's room. They had also got a new bunk bed. Aimee slept on the top and Megan on the bottom.

Although all this had been happening, they were still keeping Flower.

One night they were very close to having Flower taken away, but they were very lucky.

When they were brushing their teeth they had left Flower under the bed, then mum went in their room but Flower had learned by then to stay out of sight.

In the morning Ben came in their bedroom AND HE HAD SEEN FLOWER!

Megan and Aimee woke up; they saw Ben in the room staring in surprise at Flower. The girls told him not to say a thing. Surprisingly he didn't say a thing. That afternoon all three of them were in Megan's and Aimee's bedroom. They decided to let their parents find out about Flower themselves so they didn't have to say anything.

Chapter 6: The Secret Comes to an End.

By the next morning, their parents still hadn't noticed that there was a puppy in the house, so Megan came up with a plan for her and Aimee

"You and I are going to walk down those steps and tell them ourselves. We are not going to tell Ben and we will not get upset if she gets taken away. You are going to carry Flower down and I'll do the speaking. You got it?"

"Yes," mumbled Aimee.

Aimee picked up Flower and said, "I can't lose you as well as my Mum and Dad. We love you Flower and we will never stop".

Megan's brother was already eating breakfast downstairs. They had walked down very frightened. Megan's dad was sitting writing about work and Megan's mum was reading a book called The Girl on the Train.

Ben could see that Aimee was holding Flower, so he got out of his seat and said:

"What on earth do you girls think you're doing?"

Megan said, "We'll have to say something sooner or later."

"But you can't."

"Stay out of it, we don't want you to get involved too."

Aimee hid Flower behind her back and they both walked over to Megan's parents with confidence.

"Mum, Dad, we have something to tell you. Me and Aimee have been keeping a puppy here."

Aimee held out Flower so they could see. Then Megan's mum got up and took Flower.

Her dad was shocked he shouted:

"Why on earth were you two keeping a puppy here?!"

Megan explained how she had found her stray in the park across the road and that she had brought her home and hidden her because she knew they wouldn't let her keep her.

"It was the right thing to do, but you should of told us," said Megan's mum.

"We know," they both said together.

By now Megan's Dad had calmed down and said, "I agree with your Mum. Sorry for shouting."

Chapter 7: Happiness Once and for All

Megan's mum decided to take Flower to the vet's to see if she was microchipped.

Megan's Mum and Dad took Flower into the vet's room. Megan, Aimee and Ben had to wait outside.

The vet told them that Flower wasn't microchipped so they have no idea who she belongs to. The vet also asked if they wanted to take the puppy home or leave the puppy at the RSPCA.

Megan's mum and dad had a conversation which lasted at least 15 seconds.

They decided that they would take the puppy home.

Megan's mum and dad came out carrying Flower.

"We know were she lives," they said with a sad look on their faces.   Then, the frown turned into a smile. "She lives with us!"

Megan, Aimee and Ben were jumping up and down with joy. They were so excited. Flower was too.

They went home and that was the start of a life changing story that would never end.

THE END

42

<u>6 / Amazing Aimee.</u>

<u>By Aimee Windsor</u>

"What shall we do today?" Nutty Nigel and Rich Rebecca asked their eight-year-old daughter, Aimee.

"Can we go to the swimming pool?" Aimee replied. She loved to swim and play in the water.

"Let's get ready now," said Nutty Nigel as he quickly changed into his red swimming trunks.

However, as for Rich Rebecca, she had to carefully think about what she was going to wear.

"I think I'll wear my pink two piece, along with my silver earrings and, yes, my beautiful tanzanite ring. It will shine out quite brightly in the water and nobody else will have such a rare and precious stone.

With that all decided, the three quickly got themselves ready and made their way out to the swimming pools.

They soon arrived at the large leisure centre, paying their entrance fee to go into the swimming pool. Without wasting any time, they took their clothes to the changing rooms, keeping everything in the lockers and strapped the locker keys to their wrists.

Carefully, they walked over to the deep end of the pool and plunged into the deep, cold water.

But, oh dear, disaster struck as Rich Rebecca showed off her front crawl skills. She turned for the tenth time and the very special ring that she cherished slipped from her finger. It fell to the bottom of the pool.

"Oh, my ring!" cried Rich Rebecca. "My Royal Tanzanite Ring! It's deep, deep down at the bottom of the pool.

Quickly, Nutty Nigel gasped in as much air as he could and dived down to get the ring. But as he dove, his trunks – which were a little too big – slipped off. Seeing this, the lifeguard blew his whistle, ordering Nutty Nigel out of the pool.

"We do not allow naked people in out pool!" the lifeguard shouted, throwing Nigel a yellow float to cover him up.

"But … but, my ring!" cried Rich Rebecca.

"I will find your ring," called Aimee.

With a strong front crawl, Aimee swam the length of the pool to the deep end in no time at all.

Without wasting a moment, she took a deep breath and dived down deeper and deeper into the water. She dove so fast that she was soon touching the bottom of the pool. Carefully, she stared through her pink goggles, searching the tiled floor for the lost ring. She looked to and fro, back and forth.

Oh dear, I'll have to go up for air, Aimee thought to herself. Suddenly, she saw something. Not a sparkly tanzanite ring, but bright red shorts, Nutty Nigel's shorts. Quickly, she grabbed the red fabric and surfaced.

A loud cheer erupted in the pool as she lifted the red trunks out of the water and threw them onto the side.

Then, taking another deep breath of fresh air, she dived back underwater.

I must find Rich Rebecca's magnificent ring, she

thought. Suddenly, she saw the shimmering ring, shining through the water. Holding the last of her breath, she grabbed the ring tightly and, making sure she had a good grip, kicked up as hard as she could to surface.

"I've found your ring!" Aimee shouted after taking a breath of air. She crashed through the water, hand first, showing the sparkling ring.

"Oh you are wonderful!" cried Rich Rebecca. "Hooray for Amazing Aimee. She has saved the day!"

"Hooray!" chorused everyone in the pool. "Hooray for Amazing Aimee."

"What a clever girl I have," whispered Rich Rebecca in Aimee's ear as she hugged and kissed her. Then, she slipped the ring back on her finger, clenching her fist so it wouldn't fall off again.

"I think we had better find Nutty Nigel and tell him," said Rich Rebecca. "I do hope he is dressed now."

7 / Fireball.

By Elin Thomas

Once, there was a superhero who could shoot fire balls. He was known as Fireball.

It was said that he was so strong, he could stop a tornado from happening. He could save anyone from any bad guys.

Fireball got his power long ago, from getting brunt from a fire bug. He was actually a child, standing at 5 feet high and still going to school. His secret identity was Tom Harrison, but when he was Fireball, he wore a costume of blue and red with a fire ball on it.

Once, after he saved someone from a bad guy, he was given powered friends to help him. She was in her bedroom and the bad guy smashed the window and kidnapped her.

She was only 3 years old.

Her mum and dad called Fireball and he came straight away. With his powers, he defeated the bad guy after a long fight, and brought the girl back home.

Becoming friends with the girl and her family, somehow he gave them superpowers to help him. That came a few days later when people were stuck in a burning building. The little girl had ice powers, her mum had water powers and her dad had electric powers.

Fire and electric could not help a fire, so Fireball and the dad stayed away.

The little girl and her mummy went to the fire at the tower and used their powers of water and ice to put the fire out. They heard a person shouting for help and that they had a baby. They rushed to save the person, but then more fire came.

Thankfully, the mother and baby were saved and rushed outside the building.

Then, they had to rush to another emergency, at Fireball's school. Someone had hurt one of the teachers. By the time the superheroes got there, the person had run away. They didn't chase them, they had to help the hurt teacher.

In hospital, they found out that the person who hurt the teacher was Fireball's friend, when he was Tom

Harrison, which made him sad. This was his school, his favourite teacher.

Fireball made a promise, he would find whoever did this. But no matter where he looked, he could not find his friend. No one knew where he went and he was never seen again or hurt any one else.

<u>Challenge Stories.</u>

Every year, the children are given a challenge to write a story of a specific theme over the Christmas Holidays. The idea of the challenge is simple, the story must be their own, with their own characters, setting and plot. However, despite this freedom, they must follow a specific theme. This year's theme was to focus on someone's special ability, due to the popularity of Frozen. Does their character have a special ability, what is it, do they hide it? How did they get it? Do they use it for good or bad?

<u>1 / Superdogs.</u>

<u>By Megan Goodall</u>

Chapter 1: Four Puppies.

Once upon a time, on a cold winter's noght, in the pound four puppies were born with different mums. They were born with magical, super powers. The puppies were called Sunny, he was a golden Labrador, Misty who was a German shepherd. Jasper who was a pug and a husky named Jesse. Sunny had the power of speed, Misty had strength, Jasper could become invisible and Jesse had the power of fire.

Two weeks later, they were adopted by a little girl named Lauren, and the puppies became brothers and sisters. When they figured out they had special powers, they decided to use it for good and to keep it hidden.

Chapter 2: The Letter from Zin Zan.

When they were five years old, they received a letter

that had fallen from the sky. It said:

Dear Sunny, Misty, Jasper and Jesse,

(Those are terrible names by the way)

I'm Zin Zan, a robot dog with a cat army. Just

to let you know, I'm going to take over the

world, and no scrawny little dog can ruin my

plan.

Wahahahaha!

Zin Zan.

Chapter 3: The Rocket.

"We have to stop Zin Zan," said Sunny. "Immediately,

before he destroys us all."

As quick as a flash, they ran in a rage. Suddenly,

they saw a rocket coming from outer space.

"Watch out!" shouted Misty.

As soon as it landed, the door opened and out came

Zin Zan. Immediately, the cat army charged towards them, ready to fight. Sunny, Misty, Jasper and Jesse got their powers ready, and fought back. There was a giant between four dogs and a hundred and one cats.

Chapter 4: A Giant Battle.

Sunny started to run circles around the cat army, every time getting faster and faster.

Whilst Sunny was running circles around the cats, Jasper turned invivible and crept up on Zin Zan. Quickly, Jasper pushed Zin Zan into a puddle and, as he was a robot, BANG!. As soon as he hit the water, Zin Zan blew up in flames.

"You destroyed our master!" the cat army shouted. "We will never forgive!"

Jesse started throwing fireballs at them, sending them back.

With Sunny running around them, and Jesse throwing fireballs, so the could not escape, Misty started throwing them back into space. Those that tried to escape were beaten bavck by an invivsble Jasper, confusing them.

Soon, only the four dogs were left after beating the cat army.

Chapter 5: The Real Zin Zan.

Just as they dogs thought they had won, another rocket came down from space, and out came a giant Rottweiler.

"I am Zin Zan," the Rottweiler said. "The robot was a test, now you face the real thing."

Once again, another battle started against the real, stronger Zin Zan with a knife. As Sunny ran circles around him, Misty grabbed the knife, so none got hurt. Jesse started throwing fireballs at him, keeping back, and Jasper snuck up invisible to keep him busy. During the battle, Zin Zan was scratched in the eye, leaving a deep scar.

Zin Zan grew angry. Jesse had a plan. All dogs started pulling funny faces at Zin Zan, distracting him. With the distraction, Misty rushed up to Zin Zan and, with all her strength, knocked him down, beating him.

Victorious, locking him back into his spaceship, the team high pawed and went home to relax after their hard day.

Epilogue.

During all of this, Lauren was focused on her own thing back home. But she was worried about them being out for so long, in case something happened.

Thankfully, they all came home safe, licking her face happily.

That night, they cuddled up close to Lauren, dreaming about their next adventure.

<u>2 / Power Man</u>

<u>By Robyn Lumm</u>

Once upon a time, there lived a young boy named Ieuan, who missed his friends from high school, Robyn and James.

One day, Ieuan wet out shopping when he bumbed into two people.

"Oi, watch where you're going.!"

It was Robyn and James.

"Hi," Ieuan continued when he saw who it was. "I didn't recognize you, I haven't seen you in ages. How are you?"

"Fine thanks," Robyn replied.

"So, would you like to come over mine?" Ieuan asked.

Saying yes, all the friends went over to sleep at Ieuan's house.

While they were sleeping, there was an evil master mind at work. His name was Paddy Power. Now, Paddy was plotting to make Ieuan a villain.

Why you may ask.

When Ieuan was a young boy, his parents locked Paddy's parents in jail. Paddy was taking revenge on Ieuan. His mad scientist, Thomas Testtube, was making spider potion to secretly make them magical.

One potion could turn someone into a goblin and the other make them a superhero.

Whilst Ieuan was sleeping, Paddy Power crept into his room and let the spider of the potion out. Using a jar of flies to make the spider move, Paddy Power made the spider bite Ieuan on the arm. However, instead of his arm turning green, as he expected, Ieuan's arms began growing in size.

He was becoming a super hero.

With the changes waking him up, Ieuan saw Paddy Power and Thomas Testtube standing over him.

"You two are gonners," Ieuan suddenly said.

Gulping in fear, Paddy and Thomas quickly escaped, but they left the spider behind.

The next morning, Paddy and Thomas were back, outside Ieuan's house, challenging him. Ieuan accepted. Ieuan quickly knocked Paddy on the head, then shoved

Thomas to the ground.

They lost, and quickly escaped.

When they returned to the lab, Paddie hit Thomas over the head.

"You idiot," he said. "You are so stupid. That spider was for me. My plan was for Ieuan to be the goblin, and I was the superhero, with you as my sidekick. That way, when he defeated the Goblin Ieuan, everyone would love as as superheroes."

In the meantime, Ieuan was thinking of a new superhero name for himself. He chose one that was very fitting.

Power Man.

With his new powers, he quickly flew across the world, saving people from mutants, aliens, zombies. But, his main mission was to stop Paddy Power and Thomas Testtube.

He met them outside the Sydney Opera House. Instantly, the great battle began, one hero against two villains. Fortunately, Power Man had the strength of ten men.

Knowing they were losing, the two villains made a deal with Power Man. Promising not to attack any more, and to leave the city alone, they would remove the powers, leaving Ieuan as normal. Ieuan accepted this deal, and so it was done.

It didn't matter, since then Ieuan led a normal life, even marrying a girl named Olivia, and the two villains kept their promise. But on one of his borthdays, Ieuan's friends gave him a caged spider.

A spider they saw in his house back when it all started.

3 / Corkscrews.

By Amina Khatun

"Okay children, today's lesson will be about the Ancient Flask of Immense Power," Mrs. Ville began.

Mrs. Ville always blabbered on about useless things that I didn't even need to know about, but this had to be the most interesting thing ever.

"It's said to be still in the world somewhere," she continued. "But who knows? Maybe some repulsive street thuigs have gotten it."

"Just because they get into fights doesn't mean they are thugs!" I shouted out.

"I'll have none of that Celeste," said Mrs. Ville. "Especially from you. I don't think your grandmother would like it if you were home late due to your multiple detentions.

"And just for the record, you are to clean the blackboard after school."

At that moment, the bell rang for lunch.

"Don't think about it Celeste, I know that you can

take good care of your blind Granny, even though you are busy with detention and hockey," said my good friend Millian.

Millian has always been my best friend, although always a goodie two shoes.

After the boring school day, and detention, I was running back home only to find the leader of the deadliest street gang, the Corkscrews. She trudged up to me slowly, her long black hair blowing in the wind.

"What's your name kid?" she asked me.

"Umm, it's Celeste. But why are …?"

"So, you are the one who wants to be one of us. Tell you what chump, there are lots of others who wish to be part of our gang. So, I had a brainwave. I've set a challenge for you all. Come to 12 West Lane, six p.m. on Sunday."

After that, she juust left without saying anything further.

The next day in school, I told Millian all that happened.

"You've always looked up to them, for whatever

reason," Millian began, "but this is too far. I mean, they cause trouble and I have heard rumours about their leader. They say she had drunk from the Ancient Flask of Immense Power."

"That's an even bigger reason for me to join them," I answered back.

"You will make your poor gran have a heart attack, but I know I can't change your one track mind."

On the fateful night, I grabbed my First Aid kit, just in case, and went to where I was supposed to go.

However, when I got there, I wasn't so sure I was in the right place. It was a mansion, a well kept one too, and I couldn't see the Corkscrews anywhere. Just then, the leader came out from behind a bush.

"I see you have come chump. Well, I suppose I should show you around my place. Come on in," she whispered excitedly.

When we were inside the mansion, I was amazed. The mansion was humongous, with patterned sky blue curtains , a fluffy white rub and a majestic staircase with a shining banister. Suddenly, two girls walked in, dressed in white. No, not white, it seemed lighter than white.

"All the others have failed miserably," said the leader. "Hopefully it will not be the same story as you."

"This one has come prepared," smirked one of the white girls. "But you won't need it for the challenge. You must beat one of us in a battle of how many goals you score with a hockey stick. And no first aid kits."

As they said this, the leader threw an orange hockey stick to me. It was just the right size. I followed the three girls into a room with two blue cones placed as goal posts. I was thinking to my self how easy this would be, when one of the white girls whipped out of nowhere a dirty red hockey stick.

"Wait, I refuse to do this test if you are using that battered old thing. I'll clean it for you."

As quick as a flash, I whipped out a tub of varnish that I always kept in my coat pocket and cleaned the hockey stick so it was like new.

"That is some talent you have there," said one of the girls. "Well, forget the test, with that talent of yours you could help us no problem and become famous with your cleaning skills."

So, in the end, I became known for my cleaning skills within the gang of Corkscrews. I did it, I made it into the Corkscrews

ABOUT THE AUTHORS and their stories

(Personal information cannot be disclosed.)

All the authors involved are pupils at Pontarddulais Primary School. All of the work is their own, starting with all coming up with their own characters, setting and plot, only to begin a first draft between Christmas and Easter. During Easter, I read through all drafts, making notes of correction for the children to continue on after Easter until the end of the school term. The stories were from their own imagination, with no help from me, other than the final edit. But even that was just slight alterations to spelling and grammar, I wanted to show this is their work. Every child, ranging from 7 years of age, to 11 years show great potential of being creative writers.

Pontarddulais Primary School website:

http://www.pontarddulaisschool.ik.org/

Editor's website:

http://fox492.wix.com/mrfox

www.ingramcontent.com/pod-product-compliance
Lightning Source LLC
Chambersburg PA
CBHW071506030726
47593CB00003B/1181